Magic Pony

6. The Champion Jumper

"It's showjumping," said Natty. "We can watch it together."

"Not watch it," said the pony. "Do it! I've got it all worked out."

Natty stepped back in surprise. "You mean, me and you, do the showjumping competition?"

"That's exactly what I mean. You don't think we've done all that night-time showjumping practice for nothing do you?"

More stories about Natty and Ned, the Magic Pony!

Look out for:

**Or you could join The Petsitters Club
for more animal adventure!**

by Tessa Krailing

ELIZABETH LINDSAY

Magic Pony

6. The Champion Jumper

Illustrated by John Eastwood

For Emma

Scholastic Children's Books,
Commonwealth House, 1-19 New Oxford Street,
London WC1A 1NU, UK
a division of Scholastic Ltd
London ~ New York ~ Toronto ~ Sydney ~ Auckland

Published in the UK by Scholastic Ltd, 1998

Text copyright © Elizabeth Lindsay, 1998
Illustrations copyright © John Eastwood, 1998

ISBN 0 590 19854 8

Printed by Cox & Wyman Ltd, Reading, Berks.

2 4 6 8 10 9 7 5 3 1

Chapter 1

Be My Groom!

Natty awoke with a shiver of excitement and sat up. At the end of the bed Tabitha uncurled; the feet she was lying on were suddenly gone.

"I'm going to be a groom today," Natty cried, tossing back the duvet. It covered Tabitha like a cloud, and being a cat who liked to be cosy, she curled up again underneath. Natty looked at her clock. Ten to six. The alarm would ring in ten minutes. Already wide awake, she pressed the off button and jumped out of bed. Next she pulled back the curtains and let in the sunshine, turning quickly to the pony poster on the wall above her chest of drawers. She expected to see a handsome chestnut pony stare her straight in the eye but, to her surprise, the picture was empty.

"The magic's working," she cried. "Ned's come out of his poster. I must find him before I go."

She dropped to her hands and knees and looked under the bed.

"Ned, I'm going to a horse show with Penelope Potter and Pebbles. Penelope's asked me to be her groom." Natty hoped to find a tiny chestnut pony there.

Instead she found herself talking to the gloom and the dust balls. She wondered where else to look. "Why does everything brilliant have to happen on the same day?"

When the pony in the poster did come alive the world became a place of possibilities where anything might happen! Most often Ned was a glossy picture on the wall but with the magic, he became a real, warm, huggable pony. Sometimes he was the same size as Pebbles and sometimes as tiny as Percy, the smallest of the three china ponies on her bedroom window-sill. Most importantly Ned was her biggest secret.

She turned to look under the chest of drawers, just in case, but he wasn't there. A quick glance at the window-sill showed Esmerelda, Prince and Percy standing alone in the dazzling sunlight.

If only Ned would stop hiding and become his big self she could fling her arms around his neck and give him a hug.

Natty sat back on her haunches remembering what Jamie had said the night before. "You're bonkers to be Penelope's groom. You'll have to take orders and do what she tells you all day."

His words were said to be helpful, Natty knew that, and, from an older brother who often ignored her, it was nice. But Jamie didn't understand that taking orders was worth it if it meant she could go to the horse show.

At least that was what Natty had felt yesterday. She had thought only of grooming Pebbles and watching the showjumping. But today, now that Ned's magic was working, she herself could be riding. Not at a horse show perhaps, but there was the log to jump in Winchway Wood and lots of places to gallop. She sighed, then noticing her bedroom door was open just enough for a tiny pony to squeeze through, realized that Ned had already gone.

No one else was awake yet, although Mum had promised to get up at six to make Natty's sandwiches and see her off. She looked at the clock – she had five minutes to find him – and tiptoed on to the landing. Mum and Dad's bedroom door was shut and so was Jamie's. She peeped into the bathroom, hoping to see Ned canter across the bath mat, but the bathroom was empty.

Downstairs, the front room door was closed, but moving on she found the back room door wide open. The bang bang of the cat flap startled her. It took her a moment or two to realize that the banging wasn't Tabitha. Tabitha was upstairs under the duvet. She hurried through the living-room to the kitchen. There was not a hint of a tiny pony anywhere so she scurried back to pull the living-room curtains and looked outside. The garden was empty. If only Ned would change to his big self so she could see him. A miniature pony could be galloping anywhere.

Natty tapped impatient fingers against the window-pane. She longed for someone to help her search, but if you have a secret then you cannot tell. There was just one person Natty suspected might know of Ned's magic and that was Mr Cosby at Cosby's Magic Emporium.

When he had fetched Ned's poster from the window display on the day she bought it, she was sure Mr Cosby had winked at her.

But Mr Cosby was in town miles away so that was no help. Time ticked by and Natty knew she must hurry or be late. After all, she was going to be a groom at the horse show. She had promised Penelope, hadn't she?

From upstairs came the beep beep beep of Mum's alarm clock. She must be quick. If she kept Penelope waiting there would be trouble: even so, it was so difficult to think of missing Ned's magic. She raced for the bathroom, jumping two stairs at a time and bumped into Mum on the landing.

"Steady, Natty. I was just coming to wake you."

"Already awake," said Natty. "Can I go first in the bathroom?"

"Be quick," said Mum. "I'll go down and make your sandwiches. What kind would you like?"

"Anything." Natty was already closing the bathroom door.

By the time she had brushed her teeth and washed, Natty knew a promise must be kept. She must go to the horse show. Ned's magic would work again. She could wait until next time. She flung her towel at the rail and raced along the landing. Penelope was expecting her at the stable yard at a quarter past six. She was nearly late.

Back in her bedroom she quickly pulled on her jeans and trainers, grabbed a clean T-shirt and struggled into her sweatshirt. She was ready.

"Goodbye," she said, giving a quick pat to Percy's sun-warmed back. He was facing the window the way she had left him. "Wish me luck, you three. I've never been a groom before."

Across the lane in Pebbles' field a chestnut pony cantered towards one of Penelope's practice jumps.

"Ned," Natty gasped, and with a leap and a bound, the pony soared over it, his mane flying, no longer the tiny pony he must have been to have gone out through the cat flap. Now he was as big and as handsome as Pebbles. Spellbound, she watched him turn for a row of blue plastic barrels. The jump was magnificent.

Why hadn't he woken her up? Why had he gone off by himself? She hadn't even been able to tell him she was going to the horse show with Penelope. But more serious, if he didn't watch out, Penelope would see him. At any minute she would arrive in her stable yard.

Natty, wanting more than anything to run outside and jump on Ned's back, wished they could gallop away for a day in Winchway Wood. She took a deep breath. Why not?

She raced from her bedroom and pounded down the stairs. She was at the front door in a moment. Wrenching it open, she ran down the path and was through the gate like a whirlwind. She swung herself to the top of the field gate and was about to jump on to the grass when she saw the chestnut pony had gone. An uncomfortable feeling welled up inside her. Was Ned avoiding her? Didn't he want to be her friend any more?

Mum called from the front door. "Natty, what are you doing? Come and pack your rucksack. You're going to be late."

Natty dropped from the gate. If Ned didn't want her to find him she knew she wouldn't. She tried not to feel hurt. She would leave her bedroom window open so that he could take the easy way back to his poster by jumping up the fig-tree leaves to her window-sill. She would just have to hurry up and go. There was no other choice. Outside the stable-yard gate Penelope beckoned to her.

"Get a move on, Natty. It's twenty past six. You're supposed to give Pebbles his breakfast." Jamie was right. The day was going to be filled with a stream of orders. Oh well, she supposed it was better that than knowing Ned's magic was working and not being able to find him.

Chapter 2

To the Horse Show

Natty hurried into the house to fetch her rucksack from the hook in the cupboard under the stairs. In the kitchen, Mum was putting the finishing touches to her picnic.

"I've made plenty," she said when Natty arrived. "Hold out your hand." Natty did so and Mum put two pound coins in her palm. "Pocket money and some for an ice-cream."

"Do they have ice-creams at horse shows?"

"I don't know," said Mum. "But they might."

Natty crammed her sandwich box, a can of lemonade and a bottle of fizzy water into her rucksack.

"Here," said Mum, "and these." She added two apples and a banana. "That should keep you going."

"Thanks, Mum. There's something I've got to do upstairs. Hang on to this!" Natty thrust her rucksack into Mum's hands and raced for the stairs. She burst into her bedroom, causing a startled cat to peep from under the duvet.

"It's only me, Tabs." Natty pulled open the top drawer of her chest of drawers. "I need my purse." Unzipping it, she added the two pounds to the few coins already there before stuffing it in her pocket. Then she opened the window just enough for a tiny pony to come in and raced downstairs again to the hall.

Mum handed Natty the rucksack, planted a kiss on her forehead and pulled the front door open. "Have a nice time."

Natty ran down the path, gave Mum a wave and with a last look over the field gate hurried down the lane to the stable yard.

By the time she arrived, Pebbles had already eaten his breakfast. He was tied up outside his stable and Penelope was undoing his tail, which had spent the night cocooned in a blue bandage to keep it clean.

"Where've you been, Natty? You should have been here ages ago. You can start on the mucking out." Natty dumped her rucksack on the tackroom floor.

"Can I help with the grooming?"

"You can when you've finished." With a sigh, Natty fetched the wheelbarrow. "And fill a haynet to take in the trailer."

While Natty was busy with her

pitchfork, Mrs Potter reversed across the lane and into the yard, turning the car to stop in front of the horse trailer, ready for hitching up.

"Hello, Natty," she said when Natty wheeled the barrow past on her way to the dung heap. "Good of you to help."

By the time the stable was neat and tidy and Mrs Potter had tied the haynet inside the trailer, Penelope was looking mighty flustered.

"Wash and dry Pebbles' hooves, Natty. Then I can put on the hoof oil," she said. Natty sighed and picked up a bucket.

"Can I do the oiling?"

"Okay," said Penelope unexpectedly. "I'll put the tack in the car." And she handed over the can and the brush. "You can body-brush him, too, if you like. He could do with a bit more gloss. Then put on his travelling rug." Penelope set off for the tack room. "I'll do his tail bandage and boots." Natty grinned. At last she had something interesting to do.

"Haven't you got his rug on yet?" said Penelope, returning a few minutes later, arms full of pony travelling boots.

Natty hurried to obey. Penelope dumped the boots and pulled out a tail bandage from the waistband of her jodhpurs. She bandaged Pebbles' tail with the quick, deft movements of someone who had done it many times before.

"If you keep on being my groom you can do all this," she said. "Then I'll be able to relax and get myself ready for the jumping. Real showjumpers always have grooms. Then they can concentrate on what's important."

Tail bandage in place, Penelope started Velcroing on the travelling boots which Natty knew were necessary in case Pebbles knocked his legs in the trailer. By the time they had finished, Pebbles looked extremely smart and was ready to be loaded.

Up until this moment Natty hadn't thought how horrible it was going to be leaving Ned behind.

"Put the grooming box in the back of the car," said Penelope.

"Stand back, Natty," said Mrs Potter, giving a different order. "It can go in when I've backed round." Natty stepped out of the way while the trailer was reversed into position. She felt a thrill of excitement when Pebbles was led in and the ramp was raised. They were ready to go.

"Don't hang about," Penelope snapped. "We're off."

Natty hurried to the back of the car and, pulling open the door, found all kinds of bits and pieces. Penelope's riding clothes for a start. She pushed aside a bag of coloured bandages and slid in the grooming box. The moment she slammed the door the engine started.

"Get in," shouted Penelope from the front window. Natty climbed aboard. As soon as her bottom was in place they were off.

"Make sure you don't get Pebbles' hair everywhere, Natty. It's such a nuisance to get off the seats," said Mrs Potter. Natty did up her seat-belt and, as they drove into the lane, obligingly brushed at her legs. "Penelope, you're going to have to map read."

"Me? Why can't Natty do it?"

"Because you're sitting in the front. It's easier for me to hear."

Penelope sat in a silent smoulder; Natty slumped in her back seat. This was going to be a day to remember all right. Glancing out of the window she was surprised to see Ned trot across the stable yard. Then he was lost to view. She took a quick look to see if Mrs Potter and Penelope had seen him. No, Mrs Potter was concentrating on her driving and Penelope was struggling with the road map.

Natty stretched round to glimpse a flash of chestnut in the lane. Was Ned going to follow them? Common sense

told her it was impossible. A loose pony galloping after a horse trailer would soon attract attention. Her best hope was that by the time she came home again, Ned would be safely back in his picture.

They breezed along the open road, following Penelope's directions. "Help!" said Natty, and suddenly sat up. "I've left my rucksack in the tackroom!"

"Tough," said Penelope. "It's too late to go back for it now. You'll just have to manage without it."

Natty's tummy rumbled just to remind her of where breakfast was and she realized Jamie was right. She was bonkers. She'd missed Ned in order to be bossed all day by Penelope and now she was going to go hungry, too. She curled in her seat trying to cheer herself up with a horse-show pretend. But the only picture she could imagine was of Ned left behind in the lane watching them go.

Chapter 3

Going It Alone

It didn't take as long as Natty thought it would to drive to the show ground. They came to a white sign which read Horse Show with an arrow directing them down a narrow lane. Natty sat up not wanting to miss a thing. The show ground was a large field. It was marked out by the tops of parked lorries and the pale roof of a marquee visible above the hedge.

They drove in through the gate to find an amazing number of trailers and horseboxes parked in several long rows. There were ponies everywhere, bays, blacks, greys, roans, some tied to their vehicles, some being groomed, some ridden. It was more ponies and riders in one go than Natty could count and the most exciting bustle of getting ready she had ever seen.

Natty didn't want to miss a thing and clung on, eyes alight, as they bumped across the grass. Between the lorries and trailers she saw the bright colours of the showjumps standing ready in the showjumping ring. If only, if only, it could be me, she thought.

At last Mrs Potter found a place beside

a big, blue horsebox.

"We're next to Anneli Smythe and her lot," said Penelope. "There's Pinkers Rathbone. That must be about the stupidest name for a pony ever!"

Natty looked with curiosity at the pretty bay pony tied to the side of the horsebox and at Anneli Smythe who was undoing the pony's leg bandages. Already she felt out of place in her jeans when everyone else seemed to be wearing jodhpurs and she longed for the feel of her magic riding clothes.

Tumbling from the car, Natty came face to face with Anneli, who smiled.

"Hello," she said. "Are you a friend of Penelope's?"

Before Natty could answer Penelope butted in. "She's my groom, that's all. Come on, Natty."

"Groom! Lucky you." Anneli turned to Natty with a questioning look. "I hope she's paying you well."

"Oh, she's not paying me at all. I'm doing it because…" But Natty couldn't bring herself to say – because I've never been to horse show before. Instead she said, "…for fun." This surprised Anneli who was about to say something else when an older girl, looking much like herself, appeared around the lorry carrying a haynet.

"Hurry up, Anneli, we're deciding on our entries. You can tie this up."

Anneli pulled a face then cheerily

picked up the haynet. "Bossy older sister," she explained. "Here you are, Pinkie." She tied the haynet to the ring on the side of the lorry.

"Is that entries for the showjumping competition?" Natty asked.

"That's right. I expect I'll be doing the Junior Class. I usually do." Before Natty could ask any more questions Penelope steamed towards them.

"Natalie Deakin! You tell lies! What do you mean by leaving this in the back of the trailer? Pebbles could have caught his foot in it and had a terrible accident." Natty stared in astonishment at the rucksack Penelope held out. She knew for certain she had left it on the tack room floor. Dropping it, Penelope turned on her heel in disgust.

Natty knew there was only one possible way the rucksack could have got in the trailer. She hurried to the back ramp as Penelope led Pebbles out at the front. Ned must have put it there. But there was no sign of him, big or small, and she wondered if he was hiding amongst the straw. She looked across the busy show ground. Ned could not be his big self here. People would think he was a loose pony and rush to catch him.

"Out of the way, Natty," said Mrs Potter, all efficiency. "I want to put up the back ramp so we can tie Pebbles to it. You can keep an eye on him while Penelope and I sort out her jumping entry. Any bother, give Anneli's big sister a shout."

"Or me," said Anneli. "I can help."

"Thank you, Anneli," said Mrs Potter. Once Pebbles was secured she set off for the secretary's tent followed by a sulking Penelope.

"You're braver than me," Anneli confided. "I wouldn't be Penelope's groom for anything." And she went back to rolling her bandages. Natty gave Pebbles a pat. He seemed resigned to his wait and flicked an ear to rid himself of an annoying fly.

She stood uncertain, wanting to look for Ned, before picking up her rucksack. She was about dump it in the back of the car when from inside the trailer came a low whicker. Natty hurried up the front ramp to find the big Ned standing tacked up and ready. Over his bridle was a leather head collar and a lead rope hung neatly coiled underneath.

His mane was in tidy plaits. The rucksack slid to the floor and Natty flung her arms around the pony's chestnut neck.

"I thought I'd missed you! But you're here."

Ned nuzzled her arm with his nose.

"Careful of my plaits. I've come dressed for the occasion."

"It's showjumping," said Natty. "We can watch it together."

"Not watch it," said the pony. "Do it! I've got it all worked out."

Natty stepped back in surprise. "You mean, me and you, do the showjumping competition?"

"That's exactly what I mean. You don't think we've done all that night-time showjumping practice for nothing do you? Now ask that girl Anneli to keep an eye on Pebbles. Tell her you're going to look round the show ground."

"But…!"

"Go on, before Penelope and Mrs Potter get back."

"Right," said Natty and, hurrying outside, she jumped from the ramp.

Pebbles was dozing quietly with his head in the shade; Anneli was grooming Pinkie's tail.

"Excuse me," said Natty. The girl turned and smiled. "Could you keep an eye on Pebbles while I have a look round."

"Sure," said Anneli. "No problem." She looked over Natty's shoulder and pointed. "They're on their way back, anyway."

"Thanks very much," said Natty, catching sight of Penelope trailing a

number card. She darted back round the trailer and quickly climbed the ramp.

"Put on your rucksack and mount," said Ned. Natty pushed her arms through the straps. "And mind you don't hit your head on the roof." The moment Natty put a foot in the stirrup they heard Penelope's strident tones outside.

"What do you mean she's gone to look round?"

"Then you'll have to get Pebbles ready by yourself," said Mrs Potter.

"But Natty should be doing it. That's what she's here for." Slowly, oh so slowly, Natty eased herself up, terrified she would make a bang or a clunk before she was on Ned's back. "She's got the most awful cheek."

Crouching low, Natty slid into the saddle. The moment she was there, the familiar blast of magic wind blew and she and Ned were spun away until they were a tiny pony and a tiny rider cantering across the rubber matting floor. Ahead, a black ditch – which Natty knew was the gap between the door and the ramp – needed jumping. She leaned forward ready for take-off. Ned leapt and once on the other side charged down the ramp, taking each anti-slip bar in his stride before his final leap on to the grass and his dash for the underneath of the car. They regained their breath while Penelope's towering wellington boots brushed past on her way to collect Pebbles' saddle and bridle.

Now Natty wore magic riding clothes; a black velvet hard hat, navy blue jacket, jodhpurs and jodhpur boots. She felt behind for her rucksack but it was gone. Across Ned's back, behind the saddle, lay a pair of saddle-bags.

"Can I look inside?" she asked.

"Please, do!"

Natty stretched round and undid a buckle. Inside was her sandwich box. She looked in the other bag and found her can of lemonade, bottle of fizzy water, the two apples and banana.

"My picnic!" she cried.

"I'm glad I noticed you'd left it behind."

"Thank you, Ned." And just to check, Natty felt in the little pocket at the waistband of her jodhpurs. Yes, her purse was tucked safely away, too.

"It's time for breakfast," she said, opening the sandwich box. "Now I've got everything I need."

"Everything except an entry number," said Ned.

Natty looked alarmed. "I'd forgotten about that. How can I get one? And what will I do if Penelope sees me?"

"She won't because I have a clever plan."

"What is it?" asked Natty, wishing she could keep wearing her magic riding clothes. But the moment she dismounted and let go of the reins they would vanish.

"Breakfast first, plan after." Ned wobbled his lips around the apple that Natty offered.

"Good idea," said Natty, who was starving. She took a large bite from a sandwich and while they both chewed, she wondered what Ned's clever plan might be.

Chapter 4

Entries

"Right," said Ned, swallowing the last of his apple and peering round the black wall of car tyre. "Hold tight! It's time to put my plan into action." He trotted out from under the car into a blinding wind which spun them tall. When they walked past Pebbles they were a proper-sized pony and rider just like anyone else in the show ground. Penelope, busy tacking up, didn't give them a second glance.

"As ever, you have the perfect disguise," whispered Ned before quickening his pace.

Natty did her best rising trot as they sped between horseboxes and trailers. When they neared the white marquee, Ned slowed.

"This is where we try out the plan," he said, walking into the shade of a spreading oak tree. "At the base of my mane near the saddle you'll find a few loose hairs. Pull one out."

"But Ned…"

"Go on."

Natty chose a chestnut hair with care and quickly pulled. Ned stamped a foot and snorted.

"Did it hurt?" she asked.

"A mere pinprick. Now wind it round your finger."

Natty wound it round the first finger of her left hand, but the hair was springy and kept trying to undo. She held it with her thumb and glued her fingers together to keep it in place.

"Now get off," Ned said.

Natty dismounted and let go of the

reins expecting the riding clothes to disappear, but they didn't.

"Excellent," said the pony. "All you have to do now is tether me to the tree and you can go. But remember – if the hair falls off, the magic will vanish and so will the riding clothes. Keep the hair on your finger to keep the magic in place. That hair will work only once."

Doing the tethering and running-up of stirrups was easier said than done with such a springy hair to hold on to, but after a lot of fumbling Natty managed it.

"Well done," said Ned. "Enter in the Junior Jumping, that's the same class as Penelope's. You'll have to pay."

Natty remembered her two pounds. "I've got my purse."

"Good luck," said Ned, turning to watch her go.

The jodhpur boots were especially stiff after trainers and Natty arrived at the white marquee feeling strangely different. A notice outside said Show Secretary and, rather shyly, she joined the queue in front of the secretary's table, glad there was no one there she knew.

It was quite a jolt when Anneli and her sister took the place behind her. She kept her back to them, unable to help overhearing what they said.

"It looks like you and Penelope Potter are going to be in the same class again," said the older sister.

"Shut up, Stephy, don't remind me. At least I don't have to be bossed about like that poor girl who came as her groom." Natty felt herself go hot and pink.

"Next," said the lady behind the desk. "Next," she said again before Natty realized it was her turn.

"I'd like to enter the Junior Showjumping Class please."

"Name?"

"Natalie…" She stopped. She couldn't use her real name. "Smith," she said.

"Natalie Smith," repeated the lady, writing it down. "Pony's name."

"Ned." She wrote that down, too.

"Number twenty-seven." The lady pushed a number card and strings across the table. "That's two pounds fifty."

Two pounds fifty! Natty fumbled in her pocket for her purse. It was more than she thought and she wasn't sure she had enough money. She put the purse in her left hand. Her thumb slipped and the magic hair started to unroll. The lady tapped her pen on her clipboard. She had a queue. Natty became flustered and her face grew pinker. Managing to undo the zip at last, she picked out first one pound and then two.

"And fifty pence," said the lady.

Natty put down ten, twenty, forty, forty-two, forty-seven, forty-nine pence and the purse was empty. One end of the hair sprang free. Sweat dribbled down the back of Natty's neck; she had never felt so hot in her life. She shook the purse and one final, surprising penny rolled across the table. The lady scooped it up.

"Next."

Natty didn't dare look round. Ned's magic hair had nearly unravelled. She shoved her purse in her pocket and grabbed her number. Outside, she scooted behind the white canvas walls of the marquee where the hair finally pinged into the air. Both it and the magic riding clothes vanished.

"Hey, Natty, I've been looking for you everywhere!" As quick as anything Natty stuffed her number up her sweatshirt before turning to find Penelope storming towards her. "I've had to do everything all by myself. A fine groom you've turned out to be."

"I'm sorry. I just went for a bit of a look round. Anneli was keeping an eye on Pebbles. I thought you wouldn't mind."

"Oh, no, I don't mind, tacking up, brushing out Pebbles' tail and putting on the tendon boots all by myself when I'm supposed to have a groom. Well, you can jolly well come and finish off. I need to change."

Natty sighed and glanced to where Ned was tethered. She had no choice and trudged behind Penelope back to the trailer. From the shade of the oak tree, Ned watched her go. Natty didn't dare look back. It was obvious what had happened.

"Oh there you are, Natty," said Mrs Potter vaguely. "I wondered where you'd got to."

"I was having a look round."

Penelope flung her head back crossly. "Instead of helping me."

Natty bit her lip and looked at her trainers. Penelope had managed perfectly well without her and all the other riders seemed to be getting their own ponies ready. But it was true she hadn't helped much.

"Well get on with it."

As there was really nothing left to do, Natty decided to paint on one final coat

of hoof oil. The tin and brush were sitting invitingly in the grooming box. Pebbles swished his tail at the occasional fly while she got busy. By the time Penelope had changed, Natty had applied the finishing touch.

"I would have let you have a ride on Pebbles if you'd been a proper groom. Now I shan't." Penelope swung herself into the saddle. "I'm going to practise. The Junior Showjumping is going to start soon. If you watch, you might learn something." She turned Pebbles and set off in the direction of the showjumping ring.

"Is there somewhere to practise?" Natty asked.

"Oh, yes," said Mrs Potter. "There's a practice jump in the collecting ring. That's the place where the riders wait until it's their turn to showjump. I've time for a quick cup of tea before I make my way there. Then I'll show you if you like."

"No, it's okay. I'll find it." Natty set off in the opposite direction to Penelope.

"It's the other way," called Mrs Potter, but when Natty took no notice she shrugged and went to dig out her Thermos flask.

Natty hurried back to the oak tree where Ned was looking out for her.

"I lost the hair but it's all right. Penelope's practising in the collecting ring."

"And we must, too," Ned said.

Natty pulled out her number from underneath her sweatshirt and tied the strings around her waist so that the twenty-seven showed on her back. Next, she undid the head collar and took it off. She gasped with surprise when it disappeared into thin air.

"Sorry," said Ned. "I should have warned you, only we won't need the head collar any more."

Lifting off the saddle-bags, she found herself holding her rucksack. She leant it against the tree and pulled down the stirrup irons. The moment her bottom touched the saddle the magic riding clothes appeared with the number twenty-seven showing clearly on her back. She was ready at last.

Chapter 5

The Red Rosette

They found the collecting ring easily. It was a roped-off area next to the showjumping arena. Spectators milled about waiting for the Junior Showjumping to begin and inside the collecting ring Natty saw Penelope on Pebbles, in front of Anneli on Pinkie, queuing up for the practice jump.

Counting the jumps in the showjumping ring set her heart fluttering with excitement.

"There are nine, Ned. Nine whopping jumps! Look at the size of that wall. It's so big it's scary."

"We can do it," said Ned. "Let's practise. But remember, once we mingle with the others, I'll only be able to whisper."

"I'll whisper back," said Natty.

They went into the collecting ring to join the riders in the queue. Faces turned to look at her and Natty tried to smile but was suddenly nervous. When it was their turn, Ned set off at such a pace that Natty was almost left behind. He took off as she was still struggling to balance and she landed half-way up his neck. The practice jump clattered to the ground behind them and, to her horror, Natty found herself rolling forward, unable to stop. She somersaulted gently over Ned's shoulder to land with a bump and was left clinging to the reins, desperate not to lose her magic riding clothes in front of everyone.

"Well, held," whispered Ned.

Natty, shaky with fright, scrambled back into the saddle feeling ashamed of herself. It was only a little jump. What was it going to be like when she had the big red wall to face? Thank goodness she had managed to keep hold of the reins.

"Think what would have happened if I'd ended up on the ground in my jeans and sweatshirt," she whispered.

"Everyone would have had a big surprise," chuckled Ned. "Come on, we can do better than that."

He turned to join the queue for another go, passing Penelope and Pebbles on the way. Natty didn't miss the familiar sneer.

"Lucky Penelope doesn't know it's me."

"It's just nerves. You'll soon get over them," was Ned's whispered reply.

Natty hoped so. The last thing she wanted was for her and Ned to send all the competition jumps crashing to the ground. She watched Penelope and Pebbles clear the practice jump with ease and winced at Penelope's superior *that's how to do it* look as she cantered past. Natty took a deep breath. It was her fault Ned had knocked the jump down last time. This time they must clear it.

For their second try Natty was better prepared and they flew over.

"When we take off together it's so easy," she laughed as they cantered round in a circle. "Let's hope we can do it like this in the showjumping ring."

"We will," Ned assured her. "We will."

"Any more competitors for the Junior Jumping whose numbers aren't on the board?" a lady called.

Natty rode over to the blackboard standing by the entrance to the showjumping arena.

"I haven't put my number down," she told the lady. "It's twenty-seven."

The lady chalked up twenty-seven at the bottom of the list.

"Looks like you're going last, dear," she said as the loudspeaker crackled and an announcement began.

"The Junior Showjumping is about to begin and the first competitor to go is number eleven, Justin Spencer, riding Bongo."

A tingling sensation ran up Natty's spine and she rode Ned to the edge of the collecting ring to watch. This was it. The moment she had always longed for.

Unexpectedly, Penelope's voice boomed behind her.

"Anneli, my groom's disappeared again. You haven't seen her, have you? She's been absolutely useless. And did you see that girl on the chestnut pony fall off? How hopeless can you get?"

"What a cheek," said Ned, under his breath. Natty grew pink with embarrassment and pretended not to hear.

"Penelope, everyone falls off," said Anneli. "It's part of learning how to get better."

"I don't."

"We'll just have to wait and see about that, won't we," said Anneli. Penelope rode off in a huff.

Sometimes Penelope can be really mean, thought Natty. Still, it made her determined to do her best. She concentrated on the boy and his pony racing round the course. Bongo took out a brick at the wall and then splashed into the water. Justin Spencer collected a disappointing eight faults. He was not to be the only one. Competitor after competitor left the ring with fallen jumps behind them. Even Anneli and Pinkie knocked two bricks from the wall. Nobody seemed able to manage a clear round.

"We'll watch Penelope and then have another practice jump to put us in the mood," said Ned when it was Penelope's turn.

Pebbles trotted into the arena and Penelope urged him into a canter.

With his silver tail flowing, he cleared jump after jump until he came to the wide water. Maybe it was the shadow of a bird or maybe the water was a surprise, but whatever it was, at the last moment Pebbles stopped and skidded into the poles. He sent Penelope spiralling over his head to land with a mighty splash. By the time she stood up, she was soaked.

"Mmm," whispered Ned. "What was it Penelope said about never falling off?"

"Oh, dear," said Natty. "That's going to put her in a really bad mood."

They turned for the practice jump and Natty soon forgot about Penelope as she and Ned soared over the single pole, not once but twice. Then, before she was expecting it, her name was called over the loudspeaker.

"And the last to go in the Junior Showjumping is number twenty-seven, Natalie Smith riding Ned."

"It's us!" she gasped. "And it's scary."

"It needn't be," said Ned. "So far there are no clear rounds. All we need to do is jump without knocking anything down and we've won."

"Do you think we can do it?"

"We'll give it a jolly good try," he whispered, and trotted into the arena.

They cantered in an elegant circle waiting for the start bell to ring. Natty sat up, trying to look her best, feeling the gaze of the crowd upon her. Then the bell sounded and she glued her eyes to the first jump, an inviting rustic cross pole.

Cantering towards it, Natty felt a flutter in her tummy, yet the moment they cleared it her nerves vanished. The bigger blue and white upright was next but Natty was ready for it and even while they were in the air they began the turn that would take them to the fir-tree hedge.

Now Natty had the attention of the crowd. Ponies and riders gathered to watch this unknown girl on her chestnut pony, but Natty was too busy to notice. Having cleared the fir-tree hedge, she and Ned had the problem of the tricky double.

"It'll be jump stride jump," panted Ned. "Hang on tight."

Ned's feet pounded the grass and the first part of the double was upon them.

He leapt into the air. Natty leaned forward for the stride in the middle and they were in the air again, clearing it without mishap. Ned was going at such speed, there was hardly time to think as they turned across the arena for the parallel. Beyond its yellow and white poles loomed the giant red wall.

"Steady up, steady, Ned," Natty said as they soared over the parallel and cantered purposefully to the big red wall.

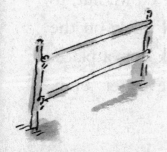

Natty was alarmed by the size of it but there was no stopping now as Ned reared up against the large rectangular bricks.

There was a gasp from the crowd but, to Natty's relief, they landed safely on the other side with not a brick out of place. Next was the race to the water jump.

The wind whistled as Ned galloped flat out. He took off with a long stretching jump, determined not to put a foot in the water. They landed well clear.

"Slow up, Ned, slow," said Natty, realising they must if they were going to get safely over the staircase which was coming up fast.

Ned had trouble steadying himself and they took off at a funny angle. This unbalanced Natty and caused Ned to rap the top pole with his hind leg. Had it fallen? Gathering up the reins, Natty didn't dare look back until they had cleared the painted barrels and raced through the finishing line. She could hardly believe it, the pole was still in place. From around the show ring the spectators applauded the only clear round. They had won.

It was Natty's best ever pretend come true when she and Ned were presented with the first prize red rosette. She clipped it proudly to Ned's bridle and led the way in the lap of honour, cantering out of the showjumping arena with applause still ringing in her ears.

Arriving back at the oak tree, Natty's face wore the widest of smiles. She dismounted, unpinned the red rosette and flung her arms around Ned's neck.

"Thank you for everything," she said.

Ned gave her an affectionate nuzzle with his nose. "You can take me back to the trailer in your rucksack," he said. "I could do with a rest."

Natty let go of the reins and her magic riding clothes vanished. So did Ned. Back in her ordinary clothes she opened the rucksack. The tiny Ned cantered from behind the oak tree and jumped inside. Natty carefully placed the red rosette beside him. Knowing Penelope must never ever see it, she did up the straps. The number twenty-seven she put in the bin on her way back to the trailer to help.

Penelope's expression was grim.

"I suppose everyone knows I fell off. Just don't mention it, that's all," she warned.

"I won't," said Natty. "I'm really sorry you did."

"I'd like to tell that girl who won a thing or two. Now she thinks she's brilliant. But she fell off in the collecting ring. If you ask me her winning was the most amazing fluke."

Anneli, who was putting a tail bandage on Pinkie, shook her head. "Rubbish, Penelope, she won because she rode well. That's all there is to it."

"You keep out of it, Anneli Smythe.

Just mind your own business." Natty hated it when Penelope was rude. She gave Anneli an apologetic smile and carefully put her rucksack in the back of the car.

Driving home was a silent affair. Natty secretly let Ned out to stretch his legs and laid the remaining apple on the floor for him to chew. Trying not to spill crumbs, she ate the last of her sandwiches. More than anything, she wanted to get home and pin the red rosette next to Ned's poster on the wall.

It was almost teatime when she left Ned to jump up the fig-tree leaves to her bedroom before dashing round to the back door to let herself in.

"Did you have a good time?" Mum asked.

"Brilliant," said Natty, noticing a delicious looking cherry cake sitting ready on a plate. "There's just one thing I've got to do and then I'll tell you all about it."

"Did Penelope win?"

"No, it was a girl called Natalie Smith riding a pony called Ned."

"Isn't Ned the name of the pony in your poster?"

"Yes, funny that," said Natty and hurried upstairs.

In her bedroom, she found Ned back in his picture and quickly pinned the red rosette next to him.

"Thank you, Ned, it was a day to remember for ever and ever."

"Who are you talking to?"

Natty swung round to find Jamie standing in the doorway with his magician's cloak draped over his shoulders and his magic wand in his hand. "And where did you get that rosette?"

"From the horse show."

"Didn't win it, did you?"

"I might have."

"Pull the other one, Natty. That's an old one of Penelope's, I bet."

"A good guess," said Natty, not saying whether it was or wasn't and, before Jamie had time to ask any more awkward questions, she hurried downstairs.

It was a relief when she could sink into an armchair and bite into a large piece of cherry cake. She chewed slowly, relishing the taste, thinking of Ned. To have a magic pony was the best thing ever! She glowed with happiness, smiled a secret smile and took another bite.

The End